I0640955

Firebrand

Firestorm

The Ancestors of Bjorn Esterday

Volume 01

Heed Warnings

February 1776

Wynter Sommers

USA Copyright © 2015 GJ dePillis

© 2015, TXu001966602 / 2015-05-08 and TXu001983965 / 2015-11-04

Library of Congress Control Number: 2020943167

Published by Pure Force Enterprises, Inc.
California, USA
Since 2002

INGRAM
INGRAM® Distribution

ISBN-13: 978-1-7184-0013-9
ISBN-10:1-7184-0013-6

DEDICATION

To those who feel strongly about truth,
justice, and the integrity of America;
your honorable actions make us proud.
To those who wonder if their daily
choices matter; your small decisions
impact generations to come.
To those everyday people who don't think
they have what it takes; when you strive
for extraordinary things, the impossible
becomes reality.
Your dreams today become our future
tomorrow.
Thank you for everything you do.

Bjorn Esterday
Was Not Born Yesterday
Series

Firebrand (15 Volumes+Conversation Station Book)
Edges (9 Stories +Conversation Station Book)
Gone (18 Stories + Conversation Station Book)

Bjorn EDGES Series
EDGES Book 1-Swift Encounter
EDGES Book 2-Rousing Attack
EDGES Book 3-One Foot Under
EDGES Book 4-Earthshake
EDGES Book 5-Broken String
EDGES Book 6-Key Witness
EDGES Book 7-Who is She?
EDGES Book 8-Vanish
EDGES Book 9-Chase or Die

Bjorn Series Alternate Reading Plan

1st	Edges Book 1		22nd	Gone Book 10
2nd	Edges Book 2		23rd	Firebrand Vol 9
3rd	Gone Book 1		24rd	Gone Book 11
4th	Firebrand Vol 1		25th	Firebrand Vol 10
5th	Edges Book 3		26th	Gone Book 12
6th	Firebrand Vol 2		27th	Gone Book 13
7th	Gone Book 2		28th	Firebrand Vol 11
8th	Gone Book 3		29th	Gone Book 14
9th	Firebrand Vol 3		30th	Firebrand Vol 12
10th	Gone Book 4		31st	Gone Book 15
11th	Firebrand Vol 4		32nd	Firebrand Vol 13
12th	Gone Book 5		33rd	Gone Book 16
13th	Gone Book 6		34th	Firebrand Vol 14
14th	Edges Book 4		35th	Gone Book 17
15th	Firebrand Vol 5		36th	Firebrand Vol15 (End)
16th	Gone Book 7		37th	Gone Book 18 (End)
17th	Firebrand Vol 6		38th	Edges Book 5
18th	Gone Book 8		39th	Edges Book 6
19th	Firebrand Vol 7		40th	Edges Book 7
20th	Gone Book 9		41st	Edges Book 8
21st	Firebrand Vol 8		42nd	Edges Book 9(End)

ACKNOWLEDGMENTS

We acknowledge those who actively build peace. We acknowledge all the selfless talent which contributed to creating meaningful tokens of consideration and sharing. We acknowledge that every person has a daily choice of right or wrong... and we thank you for choosing the right, good, honorable path filled with integrity because that is the difficult and brave path. Small choices today become lasting monuments of loving hope tomorrow.

CONTENTS

0 PREFACE

Freedom.

What is the price of being free? To what lengths will we go to secure the ability to choose our own destiny? Every great achievement starts with a simple idea. But, is "freedom" simple? If we had freedom, would we take it for granted until it was taken from us? Does freedom require structure to maintain it?

Locations

- **Philadelphia**: Home of John & Elizabeth Dunlap
- **Philadelphia**: The State House where the Declaration of Independence was signed.
- **Philadelphia**: The Inn
- Somewhere near or **around Philadelphia**: Meeting Town
- **Canada**: Where Tallman and his mother Eunice are from.
- **Rising Sun, Maryland**: Lady Sarah Wilson's Estate.

- **Dover, Delaware**: Hargreaves Home (Uncle Floyd and Jane)
- **South Carolina Colony**: Where Eliza Lucas is from
- **Susquehanna, Pennsylvania**: Where Susanna Wright is from
- **Maryland/Delaware Colonies**: Polly Mulhoolin & Button Gwinette live in open wooded area straddling both the Maryland and Delaware colonies.

1 CHAPTER 01: (MARCH 1776) Run

"Run!" Button, Polly's husband yelled urgently! "They're here!" His voice cracked hoarsely as he shouted to her from the front of their newly built log cabin situated in the middle of over a hundred remotely wooded acres betwixt Maryland and Delaware, near the southern edge of Pennsylvania. Out here on the edges of the thirteen colonies, out here in these British Americas, what some called "the big island". That means miles from their closest neighbor and too many miles from the closest town. "Run now!" Button warned in terror.

Polly snapped her head toward her husband's cries. The basket handle balanced on one wrist as she gently placed eggs from the chicken coop out back into the basket. She paused gathering chicken eggs from the rear of the cabin, stunned, not certain she heard correctly.

Perhaps this pregnancy, her first, was making her hear things. Then, she heard the howls of tribal Indian attackers. Polly ran.

She ran toward the forest where she might seek cover. Her heart pounded. She could barely gasp for breath. She raced.

Would they follow her? Would the attackers know she was missing and was it worth it to them to track her down? How many were there?

She ran still holding the basket of eggs she had started to collect for their morning breakfast. She had needed something to calm the queasiness she got in the mornings.

As she hit the perimeter of the dense forest, cataloged for the moment, she heard the first slice of the arrow sing through the air, thudding into the side of their log cabin behind her.

Button must have dumped his shaving water out front and then grabbed his other firearms. Just after Polly heard that arrow sing, Polly heard a firearm shot echo across the valley.

It was her husband mounting a one-man defense of their cabin. He had served in the King's wars and told her stories of the men he respected in battle... Brave men. Some women.

Button always mentioned the captain who went down with the ship or the General who led his men from the front instead of from behind the safer rear lines. The problem with those stories was that those men became legends because... they died.

Well, maybe not all of them, Polly reasoned as her feet clumsily negotiated the forest floor. She ducked to avoid colliding with low branches. She never found her husband's stories particularly uplifting. Her thoughts were punctuated by pangs of guilt and prayers for her husband's safety. Should she have stayed and fought? No. He wanted her to run... she did what was right. Or did she?

On she ran through this windy March morning. Further away from her cozy home. Closer to the cold unknown.

Even though the echoes of the raid on their cabin had faded, Polly hoped her husband had escaped from his attackers with some clever ruse.

She heard another shot. She paused... her lungs ached as she tried to catch her breath as quietly as she could. She listened.

No more shots.

No more yells.

No more echoes.

It must be over. Was Button lost?

She took two stumbling steps before her entire body collapsed against the rough bark of an immensely tall tree towering into the morning sky. Her cheek scratched against the bark as she forced herself to keep going.

Polly replayed the mundane events of the morning. Within those events, would there be a clue as to why they were attacked? Not an hour ago, she had mentioned to Button a rumor she heard about how the Crown, the King of England himself, was hiding behind hiring Indians to kidnap Colonists.

Button did not believe her.

2 CHAPTER 02: (FEB 1776) Getting Ready for Tea

Jane Hargreaves, bored, stared out her bedroom window. Her Uncle Floyd had purchased this home a few years ago when he first came to the colonies. Now that she has arrived, she looked out onto the passersby. This was not as bustling as London, but Jane supposed it was her new home, now.

Her Uncle Floyd did not have the wealth to buy a country estate, yet this plot of land had enough space to have fully grown trees planted by the previous owner, as well as some lovely flowers and

9

things in the garden.

No, this was not London, nor was it the countryside, but it was home. Her new much more "simple" home.

Silversmith, Jane's one and only servant she could bring with her, noticed Jane looking out the window and said, "You know, Miss Jane, my family back in Ireland were farmers. I'm sure I could get some vegetables growing out in the garden if your Uncle Floyd's butler...um...," Silversmith paused, "Witherspoon. That is his name. Family originally from Scotland... Edenbourhough, I think. Or was it Gifford? His extended family lives in New Jersey. If Witherspoon could procure me some proper tools. Well, I could try and grow some of the vegetables you enjoyed back home."

"This is home, now, Silversmith," Jane said wistfully, "We must accept that." "Yes, Miss," Silversmith replied.

"But I don't know what I would have

done without you, Silversmith. That voyage was horrid. I am still having nightmares about it." Jane confided, "I am so fortunate you decided to stay."

"Well, you are not to blame for the loss of your fortunes, Miss Jane." Silversmith comforted, "It's a blessing that your Uncle Floyd paid for our passage to come over here. T'was kind of him."

"I think," Jane said as she walked away from the window, "That Uncle Floyd gets some sort of land grant somewhere for sponsoring our voyage. Some sort of an incentive to get people to relocate to this wasteland." Jane sighed, "I do hope my cousin thrice removed enjoys my father's wealth back in England!"

"Oh, Miss Jane," Silversmith comforted, "You can't feel sad. Your father and mother, rest their souls, would have thought you'd have been married by now...and the law is the law."

"Yes. Silversmith. One must never

contradict the King of England and if he says that a daughter's inheritance must go to the nearest male relative...then that is what happened. Very law abiding it all was...to have my father's wealth sent over to somebody I have never even met."

"We have some blessings, Miss. Jane. You still have your allowance, which also allows for my salary. That's fortunate," Silversmith tried to encourage in a cheery tone.

"Yes," Jane felt a bit distracted, "we are very fortunate indeed. I have my allowance. I have an allotment for your salary. At least my father's will provided for that. Now you must get along with Uncle Floyd's butler...uh..."

"Witherspoon, Miss Jane. His name is Witherspoon," Silversmith commented. "Think of a butler who cleans spoons until the tarnish withers it all away."

"Yes. Silverspoon," Jane nodded a thank you to Silversmith. "Witherspoon, Miss Jane." Silversmith gently suggested.

Jane continued, "I must enter society, here. Now, that amorous Mr. Tweedbottom should be here soon for tea...and I believe I should encourage his attentions. Be honest, does this skirt look as if..."

Silversmith observed the skirts of her mistress and said, "No. Miss Jane. I know your Pannier It broke during our sea voyage over here... but I think what I have sewn will hold. I just..." Silversmith stopped mid-sentence.

"Go on, Silversmith," Jane encouraged. "I know you have held your tongue about my choice of company for tea..."

Silversmith replied, "If you permit me the liberty Miss Jane, I don't think you should listen to that Mr. Tweedbottom nor his comments about your dress looking odd."

"Mr. Tweedbottom, Silversmith," Jane Hargreaves corrected, "Is the fashion expert of this village Uncle Floyd calls 'home'. If Mr. Tweedbottom said my silhouette was lopsided, I must become symmetrical, once again. You see, I must be accepted to develop friendships."

"May I speak freely, Miss Jane?" Silversmith asked as she knelt down to clip off a thread from the hem of Jane's skirts.

"If you wish to give your opinion of Mr. Tweedbottom, feel free," Jane acquiesced, "after all should I marry, it will affect you, as well, Silversmith. What are your thoughts?"

Silversmith, skittered on her knees around the perimeter of Jane's skirts making sure her mistress was presentable for tea.

Silversmith, still on her knees, moved to the front of Jane, looked up and said, "Thank you, Miss. When I see Mr. Tweedbottom, I see him say you are too this or not enough that. As if he is right all the time, and you are required to realize and accept his opinions."

Jane shrugged, "He is right about many things. He has lived here longer than we have. I am lucky to have his attentions."

Silversmith rose to her feet and fetched a mirror for Miss Jane, handing it to her.

Silversmith adjusted some curls in Jane's hair as she continued, "But, Miss Jane. He is lucky to have YOUR attentions," Silversmith affirmed. "He should not insult you, even in jest, by calling you lopsided. Him, with his sneers and sarcasm. Moreover, when you mention it, he acts as a wounded victim and makes you pity him when he was the one who should be ashamed. Then, he reminds you how lucky you are to have his attentions. He says he cannot be blamed for this or that because he cannot control the world, yet he is responsible for how he chooses to act. Do we not all choose how we respond to circumstances in life that surprise us? "

Jane gazed at her perfectly styled hair and smiled as she said, "Oh, Silversmith. Perhaps we simply misunderstand his actions or the customs of the people here in Dover, Delaware." Jane shrugged, "Was that what you wanted to say?"

Silversmith shook her head as she fetched shoes for Miss Jane and knelt again as she put them on Jane's feet.

Silversmith continued, "It's as if he is in competition to have a more adverse story than his companion. You say the voyage was harsh and he says his day at the tailor shop was worse than the battles, which result in loss of life in these lands. Then, when Mr. Tweedbottom breaks a promise or doles out an inappropriate comment, he says he only did those things because YOU forced him to."

Jane interjected as she pulled up the front of her skirts so she could see the shoes on her feet, "I have pride,

Silversmith, I have told him when I am displeased with his...his...comments."

Silversmith replied as she took two colors of ribbons and held them out for Jane to select one. Jane pointed at the one in Silversmith's left hand.

Silversmith took a brooch and pinned it to the ribbon, then stood behind Jane as she tied it gently around Jane's neck to act as a necklace.

Jane did not own, after all, any heirloom jewelry. All such valuables had been given to her father's nearest male married relative upon her father's death.

Jane sighed.

She must be content to decorate herself with more simple adornments.

Silversmith continued, "And when you do say something to request he treat you properly or that he keep his word....even ten times... he nods as if he hears you, yet he does not...otherwise you would not need to ask him ten times. He insults, but when you ask him to stop, he only replies with single grunts or total silence or...or...or...he changes the subject altogether as if your opinions were never uttered."

Jane looked at herself in the mirror and said, "I am not his mother, Silversmith. What should I expect of Mr. Tweedbottom?"

Silversmith threw her hands in the air and asked, "I am so sorry, Miss Jane, but why can he not tell you how much he appreciates your invitation to tea. Or that your company is divine. Should a situation irk him, can he not speak objectively instead of blaming something to justify an offense he has committed? Why must he hide his insults behind remarks such as 'can you not make merry over a harmless comment', when it was quiet harmful? Can he tell you a story where he is not the victim? Can he not simply say, 'when such and such occurred, I wanted to do this, but instead I did that and this is what I think of those events.'? Can he not explain clearly how he will achieve a goal so that he can take on a wife of your caliber?"

Jane reaffirmed, "To be accepted, I must look fashionable and Mr. Tweedbottom is the fashion expert in this colony...and my only friend, Silversmith. If I am to attempt to gain social standing here, I must tolerate some un-pleasantries, mustn't I? Please thank Uncle Floyd's butler for helping you to make these undergarment adjustments in time for Mr. Tweedbottom's visit. Silverspoon..., was it?" Jane commented.

Silversmith explained, "I will pray God brings you a new friend....and that God help us all should he ask your Uncle Floyd for your hand in marriage."

"After losing my fortune simply because I never married, I have learned that one must marry at any cost so that I can support staff, such as you, Silversmith. Mr. Tweedbottom has a tailor shop in town... Other candidates for husband here in the colonies appear to be scarce for a penniless woman with a broken pannier, such as myself."

Silversmith sighed and then said, "Witherspoon chopped the bark from the Quercus Suber tree out back. Witherspoon said the previous owners of this home were told the trees were planted some years ago to see if they could grow in this climate. At least, that is what they told your Uncle Floyd before he bought this place. A forgotten experiment. Something wine makers need, I think. Well, those wood chips seem to fill in the silk sacs I sewed ..."

Silversmith stepped back and looked at Jane's silhouette, "I think it looks just like a whalebone birdcage pannier under those skirts, Miss Jane." She smiled pleased.

Jane asked, "It is rather heavy. How did you put it together? Did it take you long?"

"Well, it's an invention, then, isn't it?

One of a kind. You will be the envy of every other lady, here. Who else will be able to fluff their pannier until they get just the right shape? No more issues sitting too close to another lady with extra wide skirts." Silversmith laughed at her own words, " I used such tightly woven silk so the wood chips would not slip out and scratch your legs," Silversmith explained, "Your Uncle Floyd's butler, Witherspoon, boiled thin wood strips and bent them into the half-hoops yesterday morning, then he dried them over the kitchen fire last night. They were still damp this morning, but I sewed the half-hoops into a skinny pocket to keep the shape. Seven on each side. The hoops alone would not hold up the weight of your overskirts, so I sewed a bottom, making it like two sacks. One for each leg. Here are silk ties you can tie above your ankles to keep each side anchored in place. Then, Witherspoon took the *Quercus Suber* bark and chopped it up. He also carved a bumroll out of the bark."

Then," Silversmith continued, "I took

the bark bits and filled up the sacs. So, it should support the weight of your overskirts, now."

"The silhouette is important and I think it will do, Silversmith. I know you always get the latest fashions at the boutiques..." Jane said.

"Well, Miss Jane," Silversmith started, "It may be a wee bit fuller than what the lingerie shops sell in Paris, but I think here in these colonies, you'll look very fashionable. So fashionable, Mr. Tweedbottom will be hard pressed to find anything negative to say about your silhouette, now."

Jane looked at her hips and over her shoulder to observe how her skirts swayed, "A pity whalebone here is so expensive, but... Do thank Witherspoon for me. I appreciate how you both worked to solve this problem... You are inventors like my cousin George back in England."

"George Adams the first or second,

Miss Jane?" Silversmith asked, "Or are you speaking of the Hargreaves's who made that cotton spinning machine?"

"No.no.no, Silversmith. You see," Jane explained, "James Hargreaves is my Uncle Floyd's cousin. He is the one who envisioned a more effective way of spinning yarn. The *spinning Jenny*, he called it."

"I recall, now." Silversmith added. "He improved the machine Thomas High invented."

"Right! High's had six spinning wheels, and Hargreaves had eight." Jane added, "Inventions build on each other. However, I speak of my cousin George Adams, the first. For the 1771 New Year's party in London, he gave me a prototype lorgnette."

"I recall, now, Miss," said Silversmith, "None of the merchants had even seen that lorgnette, so none of the shops had it."

"Lorgnette, the French spyglass. Telescope on a stick." Jane added. "Cousin George tinkered in his music instrument shop, but when he created this lorgnette, I predicted it would become the new accessory a lady could wear to the opera...like a brooch. Oh, he loved the opera..."

"Everyone loves the opera in your family, Miss," Silversmith commented.

"Yes. Everyone except for Uncle Floyd. Perhaps it is the crowds. He would not even join Mr. Tweedbottom at tea with me. Said last night he had work to do in the library," Jane shrugged.

"Do you miss those grand parties and social circles back in England, Miss Jane? Like the New Year's Eve party ringing in 1771?" Silversmith asked as she removed some loose threads from Jane's hem.

"I do not regret the choice I made to come here. After one matures, one realizes, Silversmith, that to leave vapid parties packed with empty headed aristocrats, forces you to re-prioritize and take inventory on the talents you do have... and those which must yet to be developed...."

Silversmith threaded a needle. She added a couple of stitches to Jane's skirt and fluffed her makeshift pannier underneath. "Pardon me for asking, Miss Jane, but have you thought of marrying? Plenty fancied you back in England."

"Nay," Jane spoke clearly, "The men who fancied me, looked to me to pay their gambling debts. Some would expect me to be a dutiful wife, while my prospective husband collected mistresses. He would do this while, claiming I was his one and only. Lies..." Jane smiled, "I actually prefer being an unmarried, untitled, penniless woman without prospects of marriage, but with a distant relative in these colonies, who was kind enough to take us both in." Jane sighed and stepped away from Silversmith to gaze into the mirror, "My nobility, Silversmith, has become rather dusty... I "think the people over here take no notice of titles, so it does not matter that I now do not have one. It may be time, actually, to become a bit of a firebrand."

"Oh, you've caused some change, already by moving over here, Miss Jane," Silversmith encouraged, "but I'm sorry all your other servants left you." Silversmith added wistfully.

"Oh, they didn't leave me. They were in need of steady income. My father's heir was the only one with the funds to pay them their wages, yet he decided not to... That is why I contacted all the homes I knew who could take them in and pay their wages... I'm glad each and every one found a suitable job, but I will miss them."

Silversmith got up, "Miss Jane?" "Yes?" Jane replied.

"Not knowing him well, do you sense Mr. Tweedbottom is socially well connected, here? And would you view him as a possibility for..."

Jane answered, "Mr. Tweedbottom does seem to come up with excuses to visit me. I should not presume, but I suspect he would soon wish to ask Uncle Floyd... perhaps... well... eventually, that is, ask for my hand. Perhaps? I wouldn't want to presume, you see."

"Well, Miss Jane," Silversmith started, "If you make yourself the ideal woman of Proverbs 31, then God will send you your ideal man of Ephesians 4:29 and Titus 1:7... I think God would give you somebody better than Mr. Tweedbottom. That is, however, only my opinion, Miss Jane."

"Silversmith," Jane shook her head, "Shouldn't you check on the scones? Mr. Tweedbottom will be here soon and he should be served hot scones with your delicious fresh strawberry jam, sweetened with figs and grapes?"

Jane swished her skirts around a bit, attempting to look at herself from all angles in the mirror.

"Oh, yes, Miss Jane," Silversmith was about to leave the room and then she turned and said, "And I do not think Mr. Tweedbottom will complain about your skirt silhouette. It does rustle a bit more, but he won't notice." Silversmith looked up as she recalled, "I dressed you in the cotton chemise, then I laced you up in your stays so you'll have that fashionablestanding-up-straight rising moons posture." She smiled as she curtseyed, "'Twas worth sewing all day upstairs to get your pannier ready in time...and since Mr. Tweedbottom's lopsided comment was just two days ago, I'm sure he will be surprised to see it fixed so quickly!"

"You did an excellent Job, Silversmith," Jane patted her hips, "Oh, but with your new invention, I've lost my pockets, eh?"

"You have a pocket," Silversmith started, "I tied your pocket pouch around your waist, under the bumroll, but over the pannier. You should still feel the pouch when you slip your hand through the slit at the top of your skirts,"

Silversmith explained as Jane tried it successfully.

Jane swished happily as she spoke to herself, "You know the wider the hips, the more formal the occasion, and higher social standing, so I need to make sure it is the proper width for this tea." Jane reminded, "Mr. Tweedbottom often travels to various parts of this land to find the most current look and I wish to learn of these fashions before he shares lithographs with every woman in town." Jane continued, "I'm a bit concerned I'll look as though I'm from the 1740's. The hips do look rounded out." Jane straightened her posture.

"Marie Antoinette," Silversmith replied, "started the wide hip silhouette trend." Jane interrupted, "Oh? Are we talking of French royalty, now?"

Silversmith explained, "Your skirts are not as oblong as back in 1745. You are right. It is almost as round as a circle..."

" but not quite. You may start a new

trend over here, Miss Jane. With me at your side, I don't think you'll need fashion advice from that Mr. Tweedbottom."

"Perhaps I'll adopt the round hoop cage in my wardrobe later, Silversmith, all I need to know now is can you see my ankles?" Jane asked worried, "I don't want to give Mr. Tweedbottom the wrong impression and have him think me overly wanton."

Silversmith stood from a distance and looked carefully at the hem.

"Perfect! Thank you so much, Silversmith," Jane started, "I just know this tea will be splendid...Maybe even life changing." Jane smiled, satisfied as she strolled over to the window to gaze out on the people walking about.

From the window, she had an excellent vantage point to observe until Mr. Tweedbottom arrived.

3 CHAPTER 03: (MARCH 1776) Polly Ponders

Polly scraped a hand against the rough bark of a tree. She looked up. The trees above her seemed to tower into heaven. She looked down at her skirts. Dirty. She still held the egg basket from this morning.

Polly pondered.

She needed to keep going straight so that she would not circle back to her home and risk happening upon the men who attacked it but hours earlier. Her cabin. Their home. Was it burnt? Demolished? Or occupied by the men who attacked? Either way, she could not go back. Maybe not ever.

She needed to find some settlement, a town, something. Her husband sacrificed himself to let her live. She was duty bound to survive and find out what happened. What happened to her husband, Button?

With a deep breath of morning March air, she wondered who would launch this attack.

Nya Sverige, or New Sweden, was on the Atlantic side of this North American island. It was near the Delaware River. Back in 1638 when the Swedes first arrived, they named *Fort Christina* after the 12- year-old Swedish queen of that day. It was the first permanent European settlement.

The New Sweden Company formed in 1637, included Swedish, Dutch and

German stockholders and some Finnish who primarily traded tobacco and furs. In 1655, the Dutch took control of New Sweden.

Fort Elfsborg was built later and all the inhabitants lived peacefully with the Nanticoke Lenni Lenape, the "men of men" tribesmen, who remained. Button had told Polly that these Delaware Indians who lived near the stony country were called "*Munsee*". Those who lived down river were called "*Unami*" and those near the ocean were called "*Unalachtigo*", but they were all willing to trade, so it could not be they who attacked.

Could it?

Several who lived in the area had family back in 1681 when William Penn, an Englishman, was chartered for Pennsylvania and the three lower counties. Therefore, there was some resentment against the English still. Even Polly, an Irish born woman, resented the English, but she loved her husband.

Could this attack be the result of retribution? Punishing Polly for marrying an Englishman? Or was it punishing Button for lowering himself to marrying a common Irish servant? They did not know Polly was raised in a fine household, schooled, and well mannered. They did not know that the King's politics and laws forced her family into poverty and further forcing her to take on a servant position in an unknown land. But, out here, people were supposed to let you be... Would generations hold hostility toward a person's birth country in this modern day of 1776?

Polly recalled, the morning had started out so normal. So, every day normal.

Polly took a deep breath, pushed herself away from the tree, and convinced herself to keep running. She had to get somewhere before nightfall.

A low twiggy branch whipped across

her face, drawing a little blood.

Polly, wife and soon to be first time mother, kept running. Her mind ferreted out the mundane moments which had preceded her husband's frantic warning for her to run for her life.

Before the sun came up that morning, after she had gotten dressed and put on her shoes to go outside, she turned to Button.

He was unwrapping a brown shop paper parcel.

"I'm glad we went to town yesterday. Look at this..." He said with a smile as he unwrapped a new bore bristle shaving brush.

Excited he poured water from the pitcher into his shaving bowl and dabbed the soap just a bit. Then with his new bore bristle brush, he used circular turns to create a foam and started applying it to his stubbles growing from his neck and face.

"And what's this?" Polly asked as she examined the bundle. Out she extracted a thick heavy flat blank sheet.

"Oh, be careful with that," Button warned his wife as he walked over, face half-foamy, and rolled up the paper into a slender scroll.

"But, what is it for? If it's paper you need, you have this..." Polly indicated the newspaper, which they regularly procured in town.

"Nay, my lass," Button started, "This is vitulinum. It is calf skin scraped, stretched, dried and then powdered to make ink written on it last. It is not for everyday news. It's for something that will last."

"Why did you buy it?" Polly asked.

Button lathered up the other side of his face, then took his straight edge blade and wiped it along his shaving strap.

"We are soon to have a wee one in the house and I want to write down our story," Button explained.

"Our story?" Polly clarified as she took the rolled up scroll from him so he could use both hands to shave.

"Yes," Button walked over to Polly and gave her a light kiss, so she would get soap on her face, as well, "I want to tell our new baby—as soon as we teach him or her how to read -- how we loved each other despite the trials."

"So, why this Vitulinum?" Polly asked.

"Well," Button started as he swished his blade in the water basin, "The French call it vélin and the shop clerk called it vellum...but, I wanted something that would last."

He smiled.

Polly took the scroll and stuck it in the waistband of her apron, "I suppose one could be encouraged by our story when feeling overwhelmed..." She agreed, "After I gather the eggs, I'll determine the best place to store your vellum...and find time to scribble something on it." She put her hand on the back door. "Thank you," Polly uttered.

"For what?" Button turned to ask.

"For building the back door so I wouldn't have to go out the front and all the way around. For thinking of the baby. For thinking our story was romantic enough to write down for our wee one to hear one day." She smiled as she opened the door.

He turned and said, "If it is more helpful to have a back door, then you shall have one." He dipped his shaving rag into the water and started to wipe off his face.

"It'd be helpful," Polly started, "if you cleared off the rest of those things off from our one and only table." She stepped outside.

"I will build another table after I've finished building that crib. Wait." Button halted her, "You cannot go out to feed chickens without this..."

He handed her his Elliot 1760 Light Dragoon Flintlock pistol and a pouch of cartridges.

"On you go," he urged. "In the pockets. One cartridge is already inside. If you need another, bite it. The balls and gunpowder are in the paper cartridge. Bite the tab to expose it, Insert the cartridge into the chamber whole, and ram it into place. Close the frizzin, cock it, and then pull the trigger. You never know when a wild beast will attack the chickens and you need to defend them..."

"You are being over protective of me..." Polly protested as she put the basket down and put the firearm in one pocket and the lead balls in her other.

"I'm being over protective of both of you," Button reminded her. "Now, what would I do out here in the middle of nowhere if something were to happen to you? Either of you…" He shrugged.

4 CHAPTER 04: (FEB 1776)
Tweedbottom Heads for Tea

Mr. Tweedbottom, was lingering a few moments from Jane Hargreaves's home, in an area he knew she could not see him from her window. She had shared with him at their last tea that she sometimes looks out the window to see all the people. Something about how it reminded her of the bustling streets of London or some such nonsense.

Mr. Tweedbottom wanted to be close to Jane's home to time his arrival at tea perfectly. He looked at the town clock and knew it would strike soon.

He wondered about what to discuss at tea today. It should be something light and fun. He brought a lithograph to show her. That should take time to discuss laces and fabrics. Jane seemed to be able to talk about those things for an eternity.

Jane was new in town, and Mr. Tweedbottom was determined to become her only confidant.

He heard the chimes of the town clock. It was now the moment to start walking toward the Hargreaves residence. He was on time.

Along his stroll, Mr. Tweedbottom saw Mr. Tyler.

Mr. Bryce Aiden Tyler, Floyd Hargreaves's business partner. Floyd Hargreaves, was the owner of the home in which Jane Hargreaves was staying. Floyd Hargreaves was Jane's Uncle. Why was Mr. Tyler walking in the same direction?

Quickly Mr. Tweedbottom ducked around a corner to observe Mr. Tyler.

Mr. Tweedbottom had to think quickly. What were all the possible scenarios?

"Well," Mr. Tweedbottom stepped behind a bush to conceal himself and muttered, "Mr. Tyler could be paying a visit to Mr. Hargreaves, which would not do at all. Once received at the door, then Jane might invite him to join us at tea. Worse yet, she would send that butler to fetch Mr. Hargreaves and all four of us would have tea. No. no. no."

He took a breath, "Or, Mr. Tyler was invited to tea by Jane and I was not aware of this, in which case...that won't do at all. I must have tea with Jane alone without Jane feeling compelled to invite anybody else to tea."

No. Something must be done. At once. Jane must have tea with Mr. Tweedbottom and only Mr. Tweedbottom.

He would have to act immediately.

5 CHAPTER 05: (MARCH 1776) Polly Recalls the Mundane Morning

"Button, my love," Polly had said before she closed the back door leading to the chicken coop.

"Yes?" Button asked as he put his wet shaving cloth over his shoulder and splashed more water on his face to make sure he got all the soap off.

"I know we were married the moment my contract was fulfilled with that family..."

"Yes. The family who never realized how intelligent and well-bred you were because you were willing to hide it to be a common house servant for four years?" Button clarified, "Remember. Meeting you on that horrid voyage over here was the best thing that could have happened to me..."

"It's just that the people in the town. When they heard I was Irish and you English..." Polly's voice trailed off.

"Nonsense. It is our lives. Not theirs." Button consoled, "We are here. New home. New life. New country ...for both of us. Together. Don't listen to people steeped in politics. I am sure other Irish and English folk marry. It is none of their concern." He smiled.

"It's just that while you were shopping yesterday, I overheard them saying that Colonists were being taken if they were deemed disloyal to the King of England. Would you being married to an Irish lass be considered disloyal?" Polly asked.

"King George does not care about which nationality I have married. He doesn't know me, my dear." Button chortled, "And he is not going to personally punish me for marrying you... Is that why you wouldn't take my name? When we married? So you could protect me from gossiping strangers who might have political objections to our union?"

"It's not safe, Button." She looked down, "Because of me..." Polly sighed, "I've even heard some colonists...whole families even... disappearing."

"Nonsense. It is all rumors, Polly. Don't listen to gossip." Button shook his head.

"Nay, it's fact, Button!" Polly emphasized. "The politics of the crown make people hate me marrying you and makes them think they can kidnap colonists who don't bow to the crown to make 'em slaves."

"Polly. The thirteen colonies each run themselves. The King of England is the only one who can unite all of them to prevent chaos," Button paused, "Don't you need to gather eggs for breakfast?"

"There are no rules in this land. If it can be done, it will be done." Polly's jaw clenched, "You know slavery won't stop based on the nation you are from. If there is profit in it, the slave traders will just find an excuse to find a new source of slaves."

"Then," Button said before Polly closed the back door behind her, "then maybe you should be the one to write those rules to unite the colonies. You hid your education too long when you had to serve out that four year contact as a house servant."

"You know I couldn't afford passage to the British Americas without agreeing to be a servant," Polly defended.

"Yes," Button said, "All I'm suggesting is that you show those gossiping town folk how brilliant you are." "I'm not brilliant," Polly protested.

"How many languages do you know?"

Button smiled at her, "Exactly. What? English, German, French, and some Italian? Maybe others? Gaelic? You read the rules to determine how I could get a grant to this acreage by paying the quit rent to the Lord Proprietor by the King's indulgence in the Delaware Colony. The headright granted us fifty acres each in the Maryland Colony, which means, we have a vast cushion of land, Polly."

"It means our property straddles the boarder of Maryland and Delaware, just south of Pennsylvania." Polly corrected.

Button laid his hand on his wife's shoulder. "We are safe here, Polly. Over a hundred acres. We are east of New Castle County in Delaware and have fresh water: Head of Elk creek, Perch creek, and west of Cecil County, North of Kent County in Maryland...and I've just started to map it all out. We may actually own land in those counties."

Polly smiled, "And you still have your land in Georgia?"

Button nodded, "We will both acquire land in all the Colonies and build. We OWN this, now. Neither of us is beholden to any master nor corporation. We own this... YOU discovered how we could acquire this land, here. You essentially built this here cabin. Polly, we will continue to build a new life together for our growing family." He glanced at her abdomen, which betrayed a baby was to arrive in a few months.

"Aye, and maybe we could build another cabin after the babe is born," Polly added.

"We'll build thirty, Polly. Thirty like we've always said." He kissed her, "And then you can write a letter to the governing powers and demand the right to be left alone... and to be happy...and to have eggs for breakfast. " He grinned.

With that, Polly looked up to heaven and then walked out the back door, closing it firmly behind her.

The fog always looked peaceful in the

mornings, she thought. Polly reached into the chicken coop to collect eggs and put them gently in her basket.

Button, having finished clearing away his purchases from the general store, picked up his water basin from their one tiny table. Careful not to spill the soapy stubble-filled water, Button walked out the front door to throw the water out with a satisfying splash; the sound, which indicated he should start his day by making a splash.

With wet towel over his shoulder, he used it to wipe out the last bits of stubble from the bowl and snapped the towel back on his shoulder, slipping the empty basin under his arm. Button reached for the handle of the door, thinking about starting the fire in the fireplace to warm up the pan for the eggs.

Button froze.

Something was off.

Slowly he turned back around to look

at the still wild grasses before him. Did he see movement beneath the low fog clinging to the horizon? Over here? Or was it there? Something moved.

Running inside, Button slammed the door behind him, shouting to his wife as he scrambled for his own fowling piece.

"Run!" he shouted at Polly through the closed back door, his voice strained with rage and terror, "They're here! Run now!"

6 CHAPTER 06: (FEB 1776)
Tweedbottom Slows Down

With the Hargreaves residence in sight, Mr. Tweedbottom kept an eye on Bryce Aiden Tyler, who was heading in the same direction. Mr. Tweedbottom made certain to keep out of sight so that he was not noticed.

Suddenly, Mr. Tweedbottom saw a woman. She was one of his clients who was thinking about purchasing a new gown from him this year.

He glanced over to the Hargreaves residence and realized he was now visible if anybody was peering out of the window of the Hargreaves home...and this meant that if Jane Hargreaves were at the window, she would also see Mr. Tyler over there...

Happily but hurriedly, Mr. Tweedbottom rushed up to this woman saying, "Oh my, don't you look splendid. But you would look irresistible if you decided on a pattern for me to create for your gown this season."

"Oh, in this?" The woman replied, "I know, Mr. Tweedbottom, but I simply have no idea what color would make me the most alluring...and a woman at my age must look her best."

Quick to think on his feet, Mr. Tweedbottom looked around, and having spied a patch of meadow, walked over and picked some wildflowers of different colors. Then he returned to the lady.

He handed them to her one by one.

"The best way," Mr. Tweedbottom advised, "to find the color which suits you best is to take each of these flowers, hold them close to your face, then approach an unknown gentleman and pay him flattering compliments. One for each flower. Then see which he seems to respond to most. If he seems neutral on all flowers, simply ask him at the end which color suits you."

The woman laughed as she accepted the flowers, "This seems such an elaborate ruse to discover one's best color, Mr. Tweedbottom, but it does sound like fun." She looked around, "Now, who shall be my victim?"

"Definitely that fellow there, "Mr. Tweedbottom pointed to Bryce Aiden Tyler. "You must engage him as long as possible to be certain of the right color. And should you encounter an acquaintance of yours, I would invite her to join you and engage in conversation, as well. Tomorrow morning come into my shop and tell me of your encounter." Mr. Tweedbottom added, "Now, I must make myself scarce so as to not influence the spell you are about to cast." He took two backward steps away smiling before turning toward Jane's residence..

"What about that other man over there?" The woman pointed in the opposite direction.

Immediately, Mr. Tweedbottom returned to the woman's side with alarm. "No, no. It must be he. Over there as I originally indicated. The very first man I saw. I am the tailor. I know best. You want the most flattering color, don't you?"

Nodding with a blush, the woman acquiesced and started to walk over to Mr. Tyler, "And if I see somebody I am acquainted with walking by, I shall ask her to join us in conversation, as you suggest, Mr. Tweedbottom."

Relieved, Mr. Tweedbottom then bolted off in the direction of the Hargreaves home. He turned around to see the woman approach a very perplexed Mr. Bryce Aiden Tyler. He seemed to wave her away, but she was insistent, holding one flower up to her face and smiling.

"Good," Mr. Tweedbottom said to himself, "Now, I can have tea with Jane Hargreaves without unexpected guests."

Satisfied, Mr. Tweedbottom picked up his pace and headed directly toward the Hargreaves household.

7 CHAPTER 07: (MARCH 1776) Polly Sleeps On The Run

Polly became increasingly exhausted as she stumbled through the forest. The towering trees seemed to go on forever, but surely she must be getting closer to a road or a village of some sort.

Her mouth was dry. She was trying to get a breath. The forest canopy was becoming even more dense, so it was difficult to see the sky and ascertain the time of day.

Thinking back a few hours, she recalled hearing the attack on her cabin. She heard it. She did not see it.

She didn't know if her home was destroyed or if the invaders had simply moved in and commandeered all their belongings...including the crib Button was crafting.

Now, she started to get angry. Who would launch such an attack? What could have prompted it? Polly ignored the queasiness in the pit of her stomach.

She exhaled. If they were tracking her, they would have caught up by now. She paused a moment.

She looked around.

She was lost.

Her neck ached. Her back was sore. She picked a direction. A random direction. She looked at her feet. She had shoes. She looked at her hand. It clutched the basket of eggs she started to gather. She looked at her swollen abdomen. She had her baby. Oh...and she had that silly vellum paper in her apron strings. She was going to put that someplace...and now...what story would she write to their newborn about Button, the baby's father? She fought off a cloud of despondency and felt in her pocket. She also had her husband's firearm and extra shot.

She looked up into the tree branches above her and patches of sky beyond that...she had hope. Hope would have to keep her going.

Although the echoes of the attack had faded, the horrors of what had occurred were quite vivid and through those images she would press forward until she could not see them, anymore.

Again, she ran.

And ran.

When exhaustion made her legs shake and stomach cramp, she collapsed on the ground, panting.

She needed something to calm her stomach and there was nothing to eat in sight except for the hen eggs... She did not want to risk eating some of the greenery around her, lest she accidentally select a poisoned plant. Polly cracked an egg into her mouth, gulping it with a grimace. She was dismayed to see the remaining eggs had cracked and were leaking through the bottom of the woven basket. Quickly she gulped another egg before it completely leached out of its shell.

It had been hours by now...

She logically examined who would have a reason to attack them. In her mind flashed faces of the townsfolk she met in town who regarded her oddly once they heard her Irish brogue. But, would they retaliate with such violence? They had no enemies. None that she was aware of.

She leaned against the trunk of a tree, not realizing her hand had plopped into the basket of wet broken shells and yolks. The straw inside the basket, intended to cushion the eggs, was drenched. The liquid whites started to dry on Polly's fingers, making them itch. She pushed her matted hair out of her face, getting the raw egg on her cheek. With a viscous slime covering her hand, exhausted, Polly slipped into unconsciousness.

Polly had not noticed, nor had the strength to do anything about the trail of broken eggs, which had alerted the keen scents of a hunting wild boar, mere yards away, hunting for prey or ready to defend its territory.

Slowly, the bore became aware of this human intruder. A drop of saliva dripped off the tip of its yellow curved tusk. Its spikey fur bristled with anticipation. The hairy pig's lips curled back to reveal foamy gums and well- worn, yet still sharp teeth.

Slowly, the salivating stealthy beast's skin tingled as it's wiry hair stood on end in anticipation of an attack ...The wild pig stealthily approached Polly, still unconscious with egg on her face.

8 What Just Happened?

We met Jane, who has moved to the colonies to embrace her lack of a "future" in England. Her uncle sponsored her passage for her and one servant. Meanwhile, we also meet Polly, a pioneer woman who is forging a life with her husband in the soon to be tamed wild.

9 Did You Know...

The Revolutionary War started with a major battle at Bunker Hill, but the battle actually was closer to Boston at Breed's Hill.

Regarding slavery, Evangelicals would preach a doctrine of total emancipation during the upheaval of the Revolutionary War. In their initial drafts of Virginia's Declaration of Rights in 1776, George Mason, James Madison, and Thomas Jefferson all included a provision allowing authorities to arrest anyone who "under color of religion....disturb the peace, happiness, or safety of society."

The reason why we have a five-pointed star on the American flag and not a six-pointed star is because the six-pointed star was used in English heraldry.

Legend has it that around the year 1870, Betsy Ross (b.1752-d.1836), an upholsterer in Philadelphia, hosted George Washington along with a secret committee to create a flag design. Ross folded a paper and with a single scissor snip, demonstrated how to create a five-pointed star.

In real life, Betsy was originally named Elizabeth Griscom. She was born into a Quaker family on January 1, 1752, in the colony of Philadelphia. She was the eighth of 17 children. In 1773 she married John Ross, son of an Episcopal rector, which got Betsy thrown out of the Quaker church. The couple decided to start an upholstery shop. She ran it and John joined the militia. He died after two years of marriage.

In June 1777, she married Joseph Ashburn, a sailor, who was caught in 1782 while he was sailing in the West Indies as a Privateer. He later died in a British Prison. Betsy had two daughters with him.

Around 1783, she married John Claypoole, a Quaker who had grown up with her and had been imprisoned in England with Joseph Ashburn. Shortly after they married, the Treaty of Paris was signed, ending the Revolutionary War. They had five daughters.

The date when the design of the flag was finalized is not exact. For example, there is a painting of George Washington after the 1777 Battle of Princeton. This was finished in 1779 by the artist Charles Wilson Peale. The flag in this painting depicts six-pointed stars, unlike the five pointed stars of the Betsy Ross flag.

Others who were paid to sew an American flag include:

✓ Margaret Manning, a Philadelphia seamstresses (receipt of payment for sewing flags dated from as early as 1775)

✓ Cornelia Bridges (receipt dated 1776)

✓ Rebecca Young, whose daughter Mary Pickersgill created the flag which had later been spied through the thick of battle by Francis Scott Key. Key was inspired by that buffeted, battle worn flag to write "The Star-Spangled Banner".

Think about a time in your life when the world around you seemed as if it was going through a transformation. What small contribution could you have made which would impact your future?

What would be your "flag" which inspires somebody to write a moving song of hope and endurance? What might be your folded paper, which, with one snip, would actually create an influential design, a symbol of freedom? What simple act could you offer? There is nothing too small if offered with the heart of bettering the world around you.

10 Vocabulary

In the early 1770s, before the colonies united into the United States of America, some words and terms were used, which may be explained in this section.

Bumroll   This is a padding which was considered fashionable for women to wear to achieve a specific silhouette with their skirts.

Overskirts   When ladies would dress, they had underskirts, or skirts which whey wore underneath their outer skirts and they had overskirts, which were usually below-ankle-length skirts which would be visible and conceal the undergarments.

Spinning Jenny   This was an invention by James Hargraves to make spinning fibers more efficient. The design was also modified by Thomas High.

Lorgnette This was a contraption to improve one's vision. Some would bring these to theaters so that they could get a close up of the performers on the stage. It is similar to a modern-day binnoculars except Lorgnettes were often embellished to be a fashion accessory with formal evening attire. Additionally, one end was often on a stick-like stand so the user could hold it while resting an elbow on the ledge of an opera box to gaze upon the actors on the stage below.

Nya Sveriga The was a Swedish term for "New Sweden", one of the original areas settled.

Pannier   This was part of an underskirt, which acted as a cage on each hip to provide a structure to the overskirts worn by fashionable ladies. Frequently, the material would be made of whalebone, which was frequently difficult to obtain. Today the term is used to reference a bag or pouch on each side of a bicycle seat, which is used to hold items securely as one rides the bicycle.

ABOUT Wynter Sommers

Wynter Sommers is the pseudonym for an American writing team, which harnesses multiple skills in technology, research, history and education. Formally trained with a PhD in Education, Wynter Sommers blends academic classroom experience, with corporate sophistication, and a passion for developing more effective student insights through engaging storytelling.

Wynter Sommers has a heart to inspire creativity and develop critical thinking skills, all to encourage readers to make wise choices in life.

Wynter Sommers takes each story and weaves the plot with classic gripping elements, which endure throughout repeated readings, revealing new meanings each time the story is explored. The small choices a reader makes in real life could have a lasting effect in future generations. This set of stories shows the origin of not just Bjorn Esterday and Sarah Paradise, but of their ancestors and the sort of world which was established, which unfolded in each generation until Bjorn and Sarah met.

It is rewarding to learn of heartfelt, thought provoking conversations taking place globally about the characters of these books. Should the reader be presented with extraordinary circumstances, it is the sincerest wish that they act with honor, truth and integrity to overcome obstacles in real life whilst the reader hones skills of self-reliance and collaborative teamwork despite barriers outside of the reader's control. Wynter Sommers hopes you enjoy the other ***Bjorn Esterday Was not Born Yesterday*** stories in this series.